Farmer

Written by Clare Hibbert
Illustrated by Mike Byrne

Consultant: Sophie Stoye, a Wiltshire farmer

LADYBIRD BOOKS

UK | USA | Canada | Ireland | Australia
India | New Zealand | South Africa

Ladybird Books is part of the Penguin Random House group of companies
whose addresses can be found at global.penguinrandomhouse.com.

ladybird.com

Penguin
Random House
UK

First published 2016
001

Copyright © Ladybird Books Ltd, 2016

Ladybird and the Ladybird logo are registered trademarks owned by Ladybird Books Ltd

The moral right of the author and illustrator has been asserted

Printed in China

A CIP catalogue record for this book is available from the British Library

ISBN: 978–0–72329-472–6

Contents

What do farmers do?

Being a farmer is an important job. Farmers grow the food that we buy to eat. Look at the different kinds of work that farmers do.

Some farmers grow crops and keep animals at the same time.

Some farmers don't keep any animals.
They use their land to grow crops.

Other farmers don't grow crops. Instead, they raise
animals to give us things like eggs, milk, meat and wool.

Daily life

There is always lots of work for farmers to do to keep the farm running smoothly. Here are some of the things that they do each day.

Farmers spray their crops to protect them. Fertilizer feeds the crops. Pesticides get rid of insects.

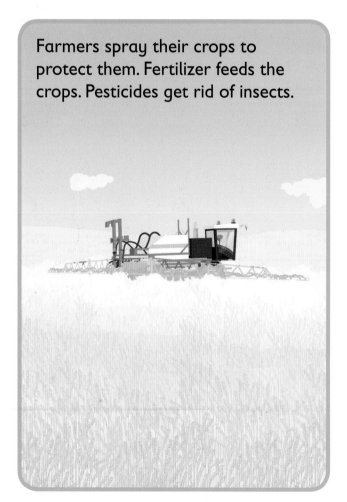

Farmers clean all their vehicles, tools and attachments. They also fix broken equipment, fences and walls.

At different times of the year, the farmer moves his animals. The farmer herds his cows or sheep to new fields to graze.

Not all farm animals eat the same things. Pigs are fed grain and lots of water.

Sometimes, baby cows (calves) are given bottles of milk to help them grow.

On the farm

Farmers often live on the farm. The farmhouse and other buildings are surrounded by fields, where animals are kept and crops are grown.

farmhouse

big barn

chicken coop

Farmers and their families live in a farmhouse. The farmer stores machines or hay in the big barn. There is a smaller barn to shelter the animals, too.

pigsty

small barn

stable

Farm animals

Farmers have to look after their animals and make sure that the animals are happy, safe and comfortable on the farm.

Cows

Cows graze out in the fields if the weather is warm. In winter, they stay inside in warm, dry barns.

Sheep

A sheep's woolly coat is called a fleece. When the farmer cuts it, this is called shearing.

Pigs

Pigs like to roll in mud. The mud gets rid of annoying flies and also helps the pigs to keep cool.

Dogs

Some farm dogs guard the farm. Other specially trained sheepdogs herd the animals.

Ducks and geese

Ducks and geese need to live near open water where they can swim.

Chickens

Chickens need somewhere warm and dry to lay their eggs.

Out in the fields

Farmers who grow crops plant cereals like wheat, barley or oats. Or they might grow vegetables such as corn or potatoes.

First, the farmer ploughs the soil. This creates furrows and prepares the soil for seeds to be planted in it.

Then the farmer sows seeds in the soil. This farmer is planting wheat seeds.

The farmer harvests the wheat with a combine harvester. The combine sorts the grain from the stalks. The stalks make straw and the grain makes flour.

Dressed for work

Farmers often work outdoors, so they need to wear practical clothes that will protect them from all kinds of weather conditions.

warm hat
This wool hat has a peak, which helps to protect a farmer from rain showers.

body warmer
This keeps a farmer warm when it is cold outside. Its pockets are also useful for carrying things like small tools or keys.

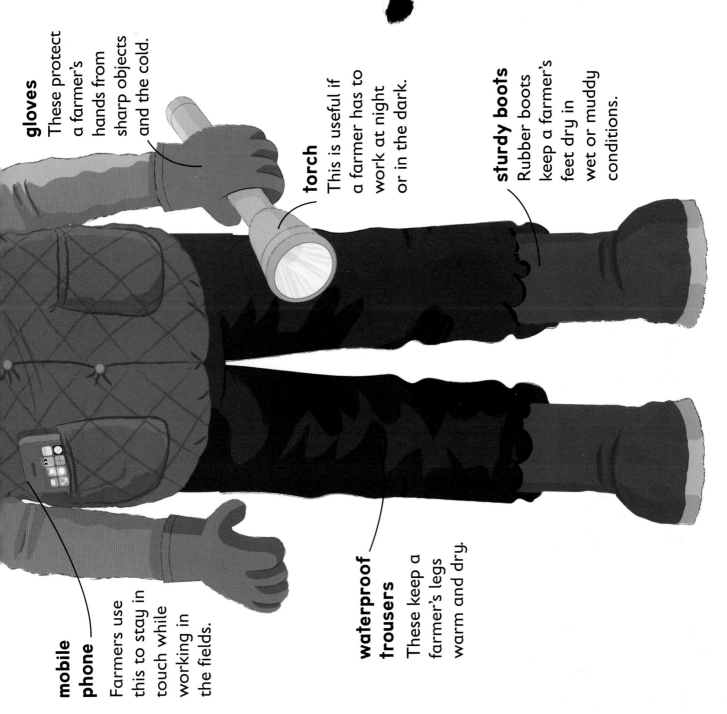

gloves
These protect a farmer's hands from sharp objects and the cold.

torch
This is useful if a farmer has to work at night or in the dark.

sturdy boots
Rubber boots keep a farmer's feet dry in wet or muddy conditions.

mobile phone
Farmers use this to stay in touch while working in the fields.

waterproof trousers
These keep a farmer's legs warm and dry.

15

Tools of the trade

Farmers use lots of different tools when they work. Some are needed for everyday farming jobs and some are more specialized.

Spray marker

Farmers mark their sheep with a number to help show which lamb belongs to which ewe.

Digging bar

Farmers use a digging bar to make holes in the ground for fences and to break up ice on troughs in winter.

Torch

Farmers must always be prepared in case of an emergency. These farmers are using torches to look for lost animals on the farm at night.

Penknife

Farmers use a penknife for jobs such as cutting open hay bales.

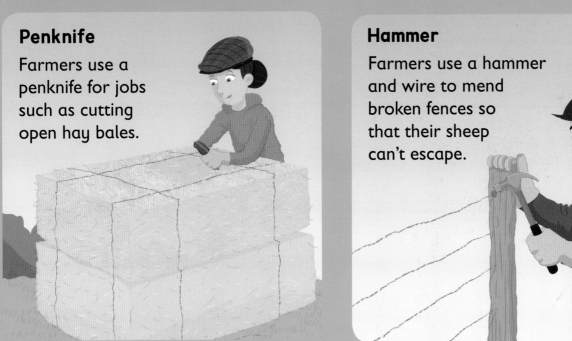

Hammer

Farmers use a hammer and wire to mend broken fences so that their sheep can't escape.

The dairy herd

Farmers usually keep cows for their milk. Some milk is sold, and some is turned into dairy foods like cream, cheese or butter.

Cows need milking twice a day. Farmers herd them into a milking parlour and connect them to milking machines. Tubes carry the milk away to cooling tanks.

tubes

milking machines

To make cream, farmers use a machine
to separate the cream from the milk.
To make butter, they use a churn to
shake the cream until it becomes butter.

butter

Some farmers make cheese from their milk. They heat the milk until it forms
solid curds and liquid whey. The curds are pressed into blocks and left to age.
The whey is drained away and used for animal feed.

whey

curds

The farmers' market

Some farmers sell their produce at a farmers' market. People often like to buy fresh food directly from the farmer.

Farmers can sell cheese, butter, eggs or honey all year round.

Different fruits and vegetables are sold when they are in season. This means spring vegetables in the spring and autumn fruits in the autumn. Some farmers make juice from their fruit and vegetables.

Moving machines

Farmers use big machines to make some jobs easier. On large farms, farmers wouldn't be able to get their work done without these machines.

Tractor and trailer

A tractor can pull heavy loads over soft ground. Farmers often add a trailer to the tractor to move animals and other heavy loads around the farm.

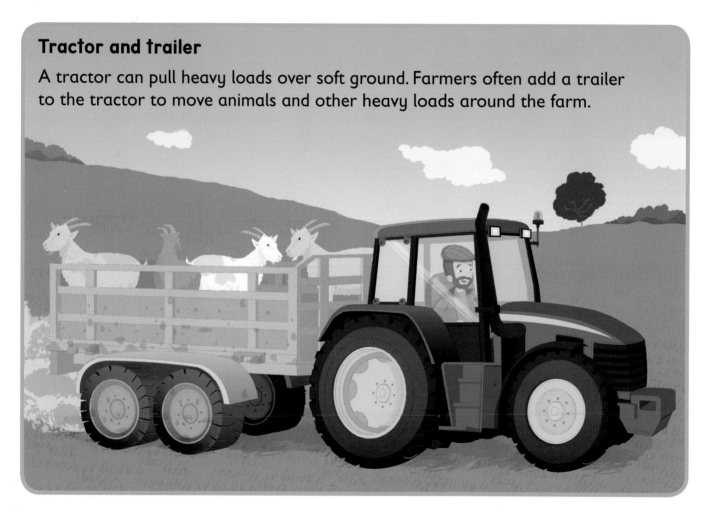

Baler

A baler collects hay that has been cut by a mower. It shapes the hay into bales and ties them up with netting or string.

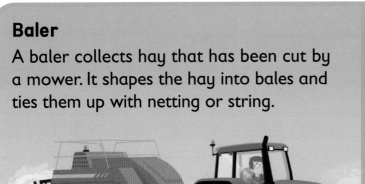

This baler makes rectangular bales.

This baler makes round bales.

Telescopic handler

Farmers use this to move heavy or large loads, such as hay bales, from one place to another.

Working together

Farmers work with other people to make sure that their animals are healthy and that the food they grow is safe for us to eat.

Vets check the health of the farm animals. They treat any injuries and diseases. They also give the animals injections that help to prevent disease.

Inspectors come to make sure the farm is safe for the workers and the animals. They inspect the machines and look at how well the animals are cared for.

At harvest time, farmers use extra workers such as fruit pickers. The workers might also help sell and transport the fruit to local shops or restaurants.

Around the world

Some of the foods we eat are not grown in the country we live in. Different crops need hot, cold or wet places to grow.

In the hot, wet tropics, farmers plant trees that produce bananas and coconuts. They also grow other crops such as coffee, tea, cocoa and sugar cane.

Farmers in places with mild winters and hot, dry summers grow olives, lemons, oranges, grapes and many different kinds of vegetables.

Places with cold winters and warm summers are good for root crops that grow underground such as potatoes, turnips, carrots and beetroot.

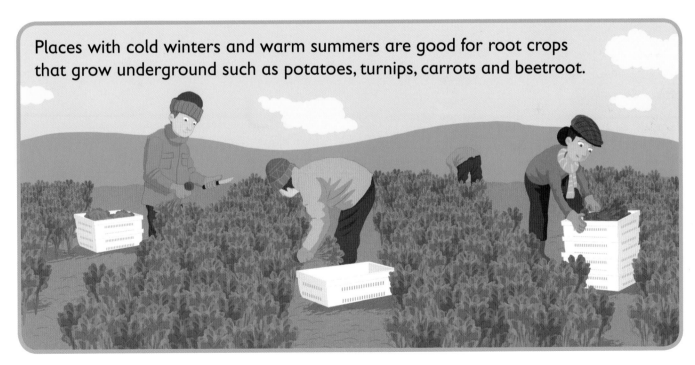

Farming through the ages

The first humans hunted animals for meat and gathered plant foods. Later on, farmers learned to raise animals and grow crops.

Ancient Egyptians

The ancient Egyptians grew wheat and barley. They dug channels so water could flow from the River Nile on to their plants and help them to grow.

Ancient Chinese

The Chinese were among the earliest people to grow rice in paddy fields on the sides of mountains. They used simple tools made from stone or animal bone.

The Maya people

The Maya lived in Central America long ago. They were among the first farmers to grow cacao trees for chocolate. They even had a god of cacao beans who they prayed to.

Being a good farmer

Being a farmer is a tough and physical job. You have to be fit, strong and happy to work outside and on your own a lot of the time.

Farmers have to be responsible. Their animals need looking after day and night – even at weekends and holidays, and in all weathers.

Farmers have to like doing lots of different jobs. Their work is very physical – which means they are tired out at the end of the day!

Farmers need to know how to operate the different vehicles safely in order to prevent any accidents around the farm.

Farmers look after the countryside. They plant flowers to attract insects and look after hedges that are home to wildlife.

Glossary

cereal A grass that produces seeds that are used for food. Wheat, barley and oats are all cereals.

combine harvester A machine that cuts down cereal crops and separates out the grain.

crop A plant that is grown for food.

curds A soft, white product that forms when milk is separated. Curds are used to make cheese.

dairy A big building where cows are milked. Milk and dairy products (foods made from milk) are processed and stored here.

fertilizer Something that is added to the soil to help plants to grow.

furrow A long, narrow dent in the ground for planting seeds in.

hay Dried grass that is used as food for farm animals such as cows.

pesticide Something that is sprayed on to crops to get rid of any pests.

sow To put seeds into the ground so they will grow into plants.

straw Dried stalks of grain that are used as food for animals such as cows.

whey The watery liquid that is left over from the curds when milk is separated.